# About the Author

Phil Clarkson, a professed day and night dreamer lives in West Sussex with his wife, two children and Betsy the dog. Phil has worked within the social work field for over twenty years and has a keen interest in human behaviour and personal development. He considers family, music, dance and football as being key to happiness.

Phil Clarkson

# Bella the Bee

Austin Macauley Publishers™
London * Cambridge * New York * Sharjah

A CIP catalogue record for this title is available from the British Library.

ISBN 9781786297846 (Paperback)
ISBN 9781786297853 (Hardback)
ISBN 9781786297860 (E-Book)
www.austinmacauley.com

First Published (2017)
Austin Macauley Publishers™ Ltd
25 Canada Square
Canary Wharf
London
E14 5LQ

# DEDICATION

For P.B.E.L

# BELLA THE BEE

Let me tell you about Bella the Bee,
who was small and chubby with a knobbly knee.
Bella lived with her sisters, mum and aunt Fee
next to the river in a very old tree.

Bella's mum would tell her, "You're
a role model for us all,
I'm so proud of how hard you're
working at school."
At the end of the year when Bella's
exams were complete,
she'd be a qualified nectar collector
for every flower in the street.

SCHOOL

Red and her wasp mates would call
Bella all sorts of names,
make up stories and exclude
her from games.
They would chant...

"Bella the Bee, Bella the Bee,
you're fat and small with a knobbly knee.
You can't fly straight, you smell funny,
you don't know flowers and can't make honey!"